Ghost horse?

"Where's your bike?"

Nickel jumped, flashed a look back at Joe, only a split second, but when he turned back, Cougar was gone.

Gone! Cougar had been right there, right in front of him, his head just inches away from Nickel's hand. In another instant they would have touched, he would have run his hand down Cougar's bony face, felt the warm breath from his velvety nose.

Or would he?

Cougar

Helen V. Griffith

Cougar

A GREENWILLOW BOOK
HarperTrophy®
An Imprint of HarperCollins*Publishers*

Harper Trophy® is a registered trademark of
HarperCollins Publishers Inc.

Cougar

Library of Congress Cataloging-in-Publication Data
Griffith, Helen V.
Cougar / by Helen V. Griffith.
p.   cm.
Summary: Starting a new life on a farm in the country, Nickel has to adjust
to the attentions of a local bully and the appearances of a ghost horse that was
supposed to have died in a fire.
ISBN 0-688-16337-8 — ISBN 0-380-73240-8 (pbk.)
[1. Horses—Fiction. 2. Animal ghosts—Fiction. 3. Ghosts—Fiction.
4. Bullies—Fiction. 5. Country life—Fiction.] I. Title.
PZ7.G881355Co 1999   98-6898
[Fic]—dc21   CIP
                                                                      AC

First Harper Trophy edition, 2001
❖
Visit us on the World Wide Web!
www.harperchildrens.com

For
Nicholas and his dad

Chapter 1

The horse came out of nowhere, out of blackness, to gallop beside the car. Nickel almost yelled, it was so sudden, so unexpected. Through the window he could see the big animal's shoulder muscles moving under its dark hide. Then it put on speed, raced ahead of the car, cut across in front of it, disappeared in the night shadows on the other side of the lane.

"Wow," Nickel said. "We could have hit it."

"Hit what?" Starla asked from the front seat.

"The horse." What did she think?

Joe, driving, looked at him in the rearview mirror. "What horse?"

The horse had run right in front of their faces. They had to be kidding him. But Nickel wasn't in a kidding mood. They'd been driving too long, and he was too hungry. So if they were waiting for an argument, too bad. Nickel just wanted to get where they were going.

They were almost there. According to Joe, this overgrown, rutted lane led to his parents' farm—the one Joe had run away from five years ago. He'd never been back. Until now.

They drove up to a white box of a house smothered in bushes, covered in vines, knee-deep in fallen leaves. Drove to the back and pulled up beside a pickup truck decorated with cats. When Joe opened the car door, the cats jumped off, streaked away. Nickel and Starla got out, followed Joe. Not to the house, though. Joe went straight for the barn, through the open door in the stone wall. Nickel smelled an old smoke smell, unpleasant, sad. He would have followed, but Joe said, "Don't come in." That's when Nickel saw that the door wasn't just open. It was gone, burned away. Inside the doorway there were only a few feet of packed earth to walk on and then a big hole where the floorboards had fallen into the barnyard below.

Joe came out of the barn looking sick. "I can't believe this."

"Your mother told you the barn burned," Starla said.

Joe shook his head. "I couldn't picture it."

Light flashed as the house door opened. A woman rushed out, calling, "Josiah, Josiah, is it you?"

They had to go through a little fuss then, the woman hanging on to Joe, dragging him in the door, Joe coming back out, beckoning to Starla and Nickel. They passed through a vestibule piled with newspapers and into a stuffy, dim kitchen.

The woman was half crying, holding Joe away

from her to look at him, hugging him again, Joe half laughing, patting her on the back when she hugged him.

A man came to the kitchen door, stood scowling. A blue TV light flickered from the room behind him. The mother was really crying now. "Lindale, look who's back."

"I see him," the man said.

Joe detached himself from his mother, faced his father. "This is just a visit," he said. "Mom wanted to meet my wife."

The man tilted his head toward Nickel. "You ain't been married long enough to grow that one."

Starla burst out laughing, the way she did a lot, bright and happy and loud. It sort of stopped everybody in their tracks. She reached out, put her arm around Nickel. "He was my sister's kid," she said. "He's ours now."

Nickel didn't like being talked about like a lost dog. "I'm Nicholas," he said to the man, "and I want to know if we're staying here or if you're going to kick us out."

There were surprised looks. Nickel was surprised, too. He hadn't meant to come out with that, but he was tired and he was hungry. He wanted to get somewhere that he belonged, even if it was a motel room, even if it was just the car.

"I'm not going to kick you out." The man turned, headed back toward the flickering TV light.

Everybody just stood there for a minute. Then Joe followed his father.

The woman looked at them sort of helplessly, as if getting them here had been her whole plan and she didn't know what to do next.

"I'll tell you what, Mrs. Clendaniel," Starla said. "I'm just about starved to death, and so is Nickel."

The woman acted like that was the best news she had ever heard. Hurried to the refrigerator. Pulled out little covered bowls, dumped things into pans, put pans on all the burners. Starla got up and tried to help, but "No," the woman said. "Just sit and rest, tell me how you are, how Josiah has been."

Starla sat. "Joe's fine. Looking for a better job."

The woman stopped working, sat heavily at the table. "I just wanted him here. His father, since Josiah left, all these years, it's been—" Her eyes teared up, overflowed. "Everything's been let go, place is a mess, and then the barn—it's been three weeks since the barn went, and he hasn't done a thing, just sits in front of that TV."

Something on the stove sizzled as it boiled over, and the woman jumped up, moved the pan, looked in it. "It's all right." Went to the door, called, "Come on out for a bite."

Between them, she and Starla set the table, dished out the odds and ends of food. Joe and his father came out, looking all right, not like they'd been arguing or anything. Joe had said they couldn't get along, that he was only making this visit because his mother had begged him so hard. Nickel was glad they weren't fighting. He wanted to stay and eat.

There wasn't much talking at the table. Nickel thought maybe so much had happened since Joe had been gone that nobody knew where to start. Then he remembered that Joe and his mother had talked by phone plenty, so that wasn't it.

Joe's mother kept apologizing about the food. "I'd have cooked a nice dinner, but I wasn't sure when to expect you." Nickel wondered what a nice dinner was to her. There was enough food here to feed an army. "And I wish I'd known about the boy." Worried to herself about where he would sleep. "There's that back bedroom," she muttered, "but it's loaded with junk."

"I can sleep anywhere," Nickel said. "On the floor. Anywhere. I don't care."

Starla laughed. "He really doesn't. He's used to everything."

"There's a couch," the man said. No smile, but Nickel could tell it was all right with him if they stayed.

Joe was acting more at home all the time. He asked some questions about the fire. His father didn't say a lot, but at least he answered. You could see that Joe's mother was relieved.

Then Joe said, "How's old Cougar?" and Nickel felt a change in the air. Joe didn't notice at first.

"Cougar's my horse," he explained to Nickel. "Meanest horse you ever saw. Except with me. He used to follow me around like a dog."

Then he felt it, too. Saw his parents' faces. His father, half angry. "Didn't you tell him?" His mother tearful, defensive. "I couldn't."

"Couldn't what?" Joe said.

Nickel had already guessed. Joe looked like he had, too, but his father said it anyway. "Cougar died in the fire."

Joe looked shocked, sorry, guilty. "Poor old Cougar," he said.

"He wouldn't come out," Joe's father said. "He was scared of the flames. I went after him, but he went farther back in. Things started falling, and I had to get out of there." No expression at all, but you could tell how bad he felt.

Joe just shook his head.

"You know how he was," Joe's father said. "You were the only one could do anything with him."

"He had funny ways," Joe's mother said.

"I know." Joe almost smiled, thinking about it. "Remember when I got the bike? How jealous he was? He hated it when I rode that bike. He would run along with me and try to nip it."

They all laughed in a sad sort of way. At least they were laughing.

"I wish you could have seen him," Joe told Nickel. "He was big, powerful. Black as night."

"Like the horse we saw on the way in," Nickel said.

The old man looked sharply at Nickel. "What horse?"

"He thought he saw a horse," Starla said, "but it was just shadows."

"It was Cougar," the man said. The word gave Nickel cold chills. The way he said it.

"You're scaring the boy." Joe's mother got up, began clearing the table. "He half scares *me*," she said, "going around here saying, 'I just saw Cougar,' or 'Old Cougar's out by the barn wall.'" She laughed nervously. "Why would a horse want to come back anyway?"

"He's looking for Josiah. He never got over looking for Josiah."

"I guess I let him down," Joe said. "Leaving him."

"You let us all down," his father said.

That kind of talk made Nickel uneasy. He didn't want any fight to start. Didn't want to be bounced out of there just when it looked like they were going to stay.

"I don't know about a ghost," he said. "I saw a horse."

"It was just a shadow," Starla insisted. "You're not used to such a country place."

Nickel looked over at Joe's father, saw that he was watching him. "Let's take a look at your couch," the man said.

Nickel followed him to the living room, where the

TV was rattling on all by itself. There was the couch, covered with pillows and newspapers. "That looks fine," Nickel said.

Joe's father looked him up and down. "Why'd you think I'd throw you out? You been thrown out before?"

Nickel started to answer, but his throat closed up. That happened sometimes. People said he was uncooperative, but it wasn't that. Just sometimes he couldn't get words past his closed throat.

The man didn't push it. "Let's go look at the back bedroom," he said. "You need something better to sleep on than that old couch."

Chapter 2

It turned out they were staying. Not just for a visit. They were moving in with Joe's parents. Nickel was glad. He'd never lived in a whole big house before with a room to himself. Joe's mom worried about how crowded it was with old furniture and junk, but Nickel didn't mind, there was still plenty of space. When he got undressed at night, he left his clothes all over the place. It made him feel like a rich kid.

Joe and Starla had to go back home, tie up loose ends, quit their jobs. Joe didn't care. He didn't like his job much anyway, warehouseman, although Starla said it kept him in good shape. But Starla was kind of sorry to leave. She'd been at the salon for two years, ever since high school, and she had clients who would miss her. "But it's probably good to move on," she said. "Good for my career."

Joe's mother took Nickel to school to get him enrolled. She drove him in the truck, but it was in walking distance of the house. He would walk from now on.

She left him, and he spent the day following kids

around, asking questions when he didn't know what to do, trying not to look lost or lonely. He didn't like being the new kid, but he was used to it. From experience he knew that he would be pretty much ignored at first. Not because the kids were unfriendly. They just didn't care about him one way or the other.

Nickel knew things would be better after gym class. Because Nickel was good at sports. Really good. And once the other kids saw what he could do, it wasn't like he was a new kid anymore. He was able to fit right in.

After school he walked home, past the new houses in the development around the new school. Joe had been surprised that the farms he grew up near were gone. He seemed sorry to see it, even though part of the reason he hadn't liked home was because there was nothing there but farms. But the main reason he left was that he and his father couldn't get along. He said the final fight was over a car. He wanted one. His father said no. So Joe left. Now he had a car. Whether it had been worth leaving home over, he never said.

Once Nickel got out of the development, he was on the old road, which had probably been fine when everything was farms and wagons, but wasn't so good for cars. It curved a lot, following the course of a small stream that had been there before anything. The road seemed even narrower than it was because of the weeds on either side reaching toward one another.

He left the road when he came to the lane that led to Joe's family's farm. It was rough, rutted, overhung with tree limbs that looked like they would fall any minute. It was a long lane, and Joe's mother said it used to be pretty, winding between big sycamore trees, lined with flowering bushes. But it hadn't been cared for in a long time, and she said it didn't take long for things to go back to nature. Nickel didn't know anything about nature, but he thought the lane was pretty the way it was.

He tried to pick out where the horse had come through the trees and run beside the car, but it was impossible. There were places where the weeds might be packed down a little, where heavy hoofs might have landed. Of course if it was a ghost horse like Joe's father said, there wouldn't be any sign anyway. But Nickel knew there weren't any ghosts. He just knew he'd seen a horse.

Then a thought, like an electric shock. What if Cougar hadn't died in the fire after all? What if he had just panicked? After Joe's father had been forced to leave him, Cougar had found a way out. But he was crazy from fear. Didn't remember who he was or where he belonged. That's why Joe's father saw him around the place. He was trying to remember.

Nickel hurried the rest of the way to the farmhouse. Some cats were enjoying the autumn sun on the back steps. Nickel thought there must be a lot of cats. He never seemed to see the same one twice.

He went into the kitchen, and there was Joe's mother. "How was school?" she asked.

Nickel said, "Fine," then asked, "Where's Mr. Clendaniel?"

Joe's mother smiled. "Why don't you call him Pop?" Nodded toward the door. "You'll find him out there poking around the barn. Then he'll come in here stinking of smoke."

"Thanks." Nickel went back outside. Came close to squashing a cat on his way down the steps. Found Joe's father down in the barnyard, just standing there smoking a cigarette.

Nickel joined him, looked where he was looking, at charred boards, twisted metal, piles of stones.

"A mess, ain't it," the man said. "Everything that was upstairs is down here now. Lucky the tractor was in the field that night."

It looked bad. Nickel was glad he had something good to tell him. "I was thinking about the horse I saw," he began.

Joe's father nodded. "Old Cougar."

"I was thinking," Nickel said. Started out slow, got more excited as he talked. "Maybe he didn't really die. Maybe he got out but he has amnesia or something."

Joe's father didn't say anything. He just watched Nickel and let him talk.

"I think he was so scared, he went crazy," Nickel went on. "But he's still hanging around the farm. You said he was always kind of wild, except with Joe. Maybe if Joe just sat outside someplace, with his favorite food or something, maybe Cougar would remember him and get tame again."

Joe's father took a deep drag on his cigarette, blew smoke out in a slow stream. "They're nice thoughts," he said. "You're a good boy."

Nickel felt proud of himself. "When Joe comes back, I'll tell him."

But Joe's father shook his head. "Cougar's gone, son. Burned up."

Nickel followed his gaze toward the sheltered part of the barnyard. The floor of the upper level had served as a roof over the area. Now there was no floor, no roof, just charred skeletons of wood littering the ground.

"He was back there," Joe's father said. "The roof had caved in on him. But I found him. What was left, I found."

Close to the smoke-streaked stone wall, surrounded by rubble, Nickel saw a long, low mound.

"I put the front-end loader on the tractor," the man said. "Dug a hole, shoved him in, covered him up." His voice turned rough.

Nickel didn't want to hear, didn't want to believe. "But you *see* him," he said.

Joe's father kept his eyes on the mound. "I thought

I was crazy," he said. "Thought it was time I was put away somewhere."

"But I saw him, too," Nickel said.

"Guess they'll have to put us both away." Joe's father flicked away his cigarette, and they left the barn together.

"Mrs. Clendaniel said you stink of smoke after you've been in the barn," Nickel said.

"Now we both do," the man said. "Call her Mom."

Chapter 3

It was pouring rain, so they couldn't go out for gym. Instead they practiced soccer moves. It was easy, even just kicking the ball around indoors like that, to see who were the real players and who were just average. Nickel liked it when there were good players. That made it more fun.

They practiced taking the ball away from each other, one kicking down the floor while the other attacked from the side, or back, or front. There was one guy, big, aggressive. He could always get the ball. When it was his turn to keep it, he could do that, too.

By the time it was their turn to pair off together, Nickel knew the guy's moves, easily kept control of the ball. When they reached the end of the room, Nickel was laughing. He always laughed when he played soccer. Probably because it was fun and exciting and he was good. The other guy didn't laugh. In fact he seemed to take the laughter personally, like an insult.

The teacher, Mr. Highfield, was enthusiastic. "Good job, Nick," he called. He was also enthusiastic if you didn't do well. "Good job, Robbo," he called to Nickel's partner.

Nickel kicked the ball to Robbo. "Your turn," he said.

Robbo didn't answer, didn't look at him, just started dribbling down the floor fast, keeping the ball close. Nickel ran alongside, saw an opening, went for it, and saw stars. Robbo had kicked him hard on the ankle, throwing Nickel off stride. Robbo kept on going, reached the end of the gym still in control of the ball.

"Good job, Robbo," Mr. Highfield called. "Good job, Nick, but try to stick a little closer next time."

Nickel looked at the teacher. Was he going to let Robbo get away with that? Some of the kids knew what had happened. He could see them trying not to look like they were watching. Well, if they were waiting for him to react, they were going to be disappointed. He walked over to his next partner, not letting himself limp. Pretty soon he was laughing again. But he decided to keep away from Robbo.

Chapter 4

Joe and Starla showed up, the car loaded with odds and ends of junk. Luckily they hadn't been together long enough to collect much, and Nickel sure didn't have many possessions. It still made a pile, though. Starla said she'd been afraid Joe might decide she wouldn't fit and leave her behind. "Or maybe tie me to the roof of the car," she said, laughing. "Or make me follow along on Nickel's bike."

He had wondered if they would bring his bike. Hadn't wanted to ask, because it would probably be too much trouble. It was really too small for him now anyway, but it was good to have a bike. They had tied it on top of the car. Joe's father shook his head when he saw it. "Miracle it stayed put," he said.

Joe started to look mad. Stopped himself. "We almost didn't bring it," he said. "I was thinking Nickel could have my old bike. But maybe you got rid of it."

"It was in the barn." That settled that.

Nickel carried his things to his room. Clothes, mostly. He had moved a lot in the last few years, and each move left him with less stuff. He was glad. It was easier when you didn't have much to lug around.

But he'd never landed in a place like this before. It felt different from his other homes. He wanted to stay. He hoped Joe and his father wouldn't get into any fights. That would be the only thing that could mess this up.

He laid his clothes in drawers, put his other junk on the bureau, couple games, couple books. Stood looking around, feeling good. Went to the window, looked out at the rest of them still unloading the car. Except Joe's father. He was looking toward the barn, or just beyond it, where the weeds grew high and thick. Where a black horse moved restlessly, wheeled away, disappeared.

It was too quick. Had he really seen a horse? Had he seen Cougar again?

Joe's father saw him looking out the window. Waved. He didn't act like somebody who had just seen a ghost. Nickel waved back. Knew that whatever had been there had been seen by him alone. Knew and shivered.

Chapter 5

The next day Nickel rode his bike to school. He felt a little funny because it wasn't a full-size bike, but it was quicker than walking.

Today the weather was good. They went outside for gym, and Nickel saw how Robbo dominated the field and the game. He did a lot of yelling as he played, orders to his teammates, insults to the other team, shouts of disgust if a player made a mistake. But Robbo was good. And he was usually right, so he got away with it.

But Nickel was good, too, and, as the game went on, he had chances to show it. He noticed that Robbo didn't look too happy. As they left the field, he edged over to Nickel. "What was so funny out there?"

Nickel knew he must have been smiling or laughing the way he did when he played soccer. Or any sport. But he didn't have to explain that. So he said, "Nothing."

"That's right. Nothing's funny." Robbo made it sound like a threat. But what did he mean? That Nickel wasn't supposed to laugh? Well, too bad. He walked faster, away from Robbo. If he wanted trouble, he could go look for it somewhere else. Nickel was tired of trouble.

The next time they played, Robbo was on the opposing team. Still yelling directions, trying to run everybody else, playing rough. But Nickel was quicker, more agile. He played smarter, and he knew it. Even in the midst of all the action, Nickel felt that he could see the whole field, see everybody's position, almost feel their next move. That was why he was good. He always had a complete picture of the field in his head, and it changed as conditions changed.

But while Robbo yelled and cursed, the game affected Nickel a whole different way. If he made a good play, he laughed. If he missed, even while he apologized or shouted in disgust, he was smiling. Any good play, even by the other team, brought a delighted yell out of him. He couldn't help it. He loved being out there on the field, so whatever happened was fun.

Until he began to tangle with Robbo. Nickel saw right away that Robbo had to be the star. And he was. In any fight over the ball, Robbo won. In any race down the field, Robbo took over and made the goal. Nickel began to see that it wasn't just skill that made Robbo come out on top. He saw guys hold back when Robbo approached. Sometimes they actually seemed to give up the ball to him. Nickel remembered how

Robbo had kicked him that first time they played together. In fact, his leg was still sore. So he thought he knew why nobody wanted to challenge him. Robbo was good, but he was also mean. You could get hurt playing against Robbo.

Even though Nickel was on to Robbo, on the alert, Robbo got him. Nickel was fighting toward the goal, ready to send the ball in, when something hit him hard behind the knee. His leg buckled. He fell on his side. The goal was lost, the other team got control of the ball.

"You okay, Nick?" Mr. Highfield called. "Good boy," he said, as Nickel jumped to his feet. "You just got a little too excited there."

Nickel felt like arguing, made himself keep quiet. What was the matter with the guy? Didn't he know what had just happened? Nickel had been tripped, knocked down. There should be a penalty.

Nickel hadn't seen who did it, but he knew who it had to be. Even though they were on the same team today and the missed goal hurt them both, Robbo wanted the ball. He wanted to make the goal. He was willing to give up the whole game just to keep Nickel from looking good.

Nickel couldn't concentrate after that. He was too mad. He missed a chance to take the ball, let it go right by.

"Wake up, dope," Robbo yelled.

Some of the other guys yelled at him, too, but a lot didn't. Nickel had a feeling that everybody in the gym class knew what was going on. Maybe every kid had to go through this with Robbo. Until they caved in. Let Robbo have it his own way.

Every day the teacher split up the class differently. His idea was to give everybody a chance to play against everybody else and to experience every position on a soccer team. But no matter how he split the class, Robbo's team nearly always won. Partly because Robbo was a very good soccer player. But that wasn't the only thing. His dirty playing intimidated the other team. And Robbo's team was psyched, knowing before the game started that they would probably win.

There were two kids Nickel had gotten friendly with, Logan and Tyler. At lunch they talked about the Robbo problem.

"Everybody knows what he's doing," Tyler said.

"Too bad Mr. Highfield doesn't," Nickel said.

The other kid, Logan, frowned. "We don't know whether he has eye trouble or he just doesn't believe what he's seeing."

"Or if he's scared," Tyler said. "Robbo's kind of scary." He scowled and held his arms elbows out, gorilla style. "Uh, uh," he said, and they all laughed.

So they had seen Robbo knock him down. Nickel had been sure that was who it was anyway, but now he had witnesses. Not that that changed anything.

But at least he knew he wasn't imagining things.

That made him think of the horse. He wasn't imagining that, either. Pop had seen it, too, called it a ghost horse, but so far nothing had convinced Nickel that it wasn't a real live animal. It had never done anything ghostly, like dissolving in a puff of smoke or fading away like mist.

"Do you believe in ghosts?" Nickel asked before he thought. Then wished he hadn't, because both kids looked at him funny.

Tyler just said, "No," but Logan said, "Why?"

Well, he'd started it. Might as well finish. "There's this horse that hangs around where I live. Pop says it's a ghost horse."

"Cool." Both boys looked interested, whether they believed or not.

"It was supposed to have burned up in a fire a few weeks ago," Nickel said. "But it's still around."

"Have you seen it?" Tyler asked, wide eyed.

"I've seen a horse. I don't know if it's a ghost. I never saw the horse while it was alive."

"Hey," Logan said, "is your pop Mr. Clendaniel? The guy whose barn burned down?"

Nickel hesitated. Decided not to try to explain the real relationship. "Yeah. But I didn't live here then. I didn't know Cougar."

"Was that his name? Robbo tried to ride him once." Logan laughed.

"Yeah." Tyler laughed, too. "He held out an apple

to get him close, and then he threw a rope around his neck."

"Cougar took off, but Robbo had the rope twisted around his hand. He got flipped off his feet and dragged before he could get loose," Logan said.

"He was all scraped up," Tyler said. "Clothes ripped to pieces. He told us not to tell anybody what happened. And from then on, every time he saw Cougar he threw rocks at him. It got so when Cougar saw him coming he would take off to the other side of the field."

So Nickel and Cougar had something in common. They both wanted to keep as far away from Robbo as they could get.

Chapter 6

Nickel hadn't been at the school a week before he had taken the best-player title away from Robbo. Nobody said it, but he could see it. Feel it. The way the kids acted. The way the teacher acted. Mr. Highfield automatically said, "Good job," to every play anyone made, but his "Good job" to Nickel had more feeling in it. Sometimes he even said, "*Great* job." It was kind of funny, but since Nickel laughed while he played anyway, Mr. Highfield never knew he was being laughed at.

Robbo did his best to make Nickel look bad. Once he threw himself on the ground with a fake yell of pain. Claimed Nickel had rammed him. Nickel denied it. Mr. Highfield told them all to settle down, let it go. Robbo looked ready to kill.

Later Logan said, "You're Mr. Highfield's favorite now. He'll let you get away with things."

"I didn't ram Robbo," Nickel said.

"Yeah, but now you can." Logan gave him a devilish look.

Nickel shook his head. "I just want to play sports,

not rule the world."

"Well, Robbo wants to rule the world," Logan said. "Or this school anyway. You'd better watch out."

"I'm not afraid of Robbo," Nickel said. But thought that maybe he was.

Nickel was getting good at avoiding Robbo's dirty tricks. So good that Robbo had to try harder. The coach noticed. Told him to cut it out.

That day after school Nickel found that the tires on his bike were flat as pancakes. It couldn't be ridden. He had to walk it home, not easy on those tires, seemed like it took forever.

It didn't help that Robbo and some of his pals followed him, swerving their bikes back and forth in front of one another, laughing in a way that made him nervous, made him think they must have let the air out of his tires.

He was relieved when he got through the development and the guys drifted off. They all lived in the new houses near the school.

Nickel walked the bike along the old road and turned into the farm lane. Ruts and tree roots made it slow going. Even with good tires, it was a rough ride. Now he almost had to carry the bike over the bumpy ground.

In the lane it was like being in a tunnel. The turning leaves made the air look yellow. Except for crow caws, it was quiet. But as Nickel struggled down the lane with the bike, he sensed movement along the fence line, felt that something on the other side of the fence was keeping pace with him. There was no sound. No rustling or crackling of leaves or sticks. But Nickel was sure something was there. He tried to see through the thicket of wild rosebushes, grapevines, honeysuckle that grew along the fence. Looked so hard that he lost his grip when the bike hit a root. Dropped the bike and fell on top of it. As he fell, he caught a glimpse, an instant's worth of look, at the black horse. A live horse. It couldn't be a ghost, it was too real.

"Wait," Nickel yelled, even before he had hit the ground. "Wait," he yelled as he untangled himself.

It didn't wait. Nickel ran to the fence line, forced his way in, ripping through vines, letting thorns scratch, still yelling, "Wait." When he made it through, the field was empty. Just weeds. And crows that took off cawing.

Nickel couldn't believe it, kept looking, as if a horse could hide. He had seen it. It had been right here. But it wasn't here now.

When Nickel got home, he asked Pop if he had a bicycle pump, but the man took one look at the tires and said forget it. "They've been slit," he said. He showed Nickel the damage, asked, "Somebody at school don't like you?"

Nickel was silent, his throat tight. He remembered

27

what Tyler and Logan had told him. "Did you ever see kids messing around with Cougar?" he asked.

Pop looked at him thoughtfully. Seemed to see the connection right away. "Big, mean-looking kid," he said. "I could never catch him."

Nickel considered telling Pop about today, about seeing a horse. Told him about the day Joe and Starla moved in, instead, how he'd seen the horse from his window while they were unloading the car.

Pop nodded. "I remember. I had a feeling. Didn't see nothing, though."

"I thought I did," Nickel said, "but it was too quick." Decided to try to talk about today after all. "He was with me going along the lane. I just got glimpses. Then he was gone."

"I used to see him right along," Pop said. "Till you came."

Nickel looked at Pop, wondering what he was getting at. Pop didn't seem too sure himself.

"All this time he's been waiting for Josiah. He put up with me, but he wanted Josiah."

"Joe didn't even see him that night," Nickel said.

"No," Pop said. "You did. Cougar's *your* horse now."

It sounded crazy. Nickel didn't know what to say. "What do you do with a ghost horse?"

"I guess he'll let you know." Pop never joked. He must mean it.

***

Joe was burned up about the slit tires, wanted to do something, but Nickel insisted it was just a joke, wouldn't happen again. He didn't want Joe up at school, yelling at everybody. Joe could get pretty mad.

He and Starla had found jobs, Starla at a salon out on the highway. They loved her already. "I was always talented with hair," she told Joe's mother. Offered to do hers and then did. It made her look younger, they all said. Joe's mother said, "What do I want to look younger for?" but Nickel saw her looking at herself in the hall mirror.

Joe was working at a service station, said he was still looking for something better, but he liked it there, Nickel could tell. So why look for something else? He brought home new tires for Nickel's bike, put them on, expected him to go back to riding to school. Nickel didn't have a good feeling about it. They'd probably get slit again. He'd have to keep it quiet somehow, or Joe would be up at school looking to break somebody's arms.

At first there hadn't seemed to be much to do at Joe's parents' place. Nickel watched a lot of TV, talked to Mom, ate way too much. Then Pop asked for his help cleaning out one of the outbuildings to make a shed for the tractor. Nickel liked doing it. It felt good using his muscles. He began following Pop around as he worked, helping, and learning about the farm, where the stream ran, what fields were planted now, which ones were waiting for spring.

One day Pop showed him how to run the tractor, let him drive around awhile, told him he'd hitch the snowplow to it this winter so Nickel could plow the lane. Nickel found himself wishing for snow in October.

No animals, except for those cats. Nickel had thought a farm always had animals, but Pop said with just himself it was too much work. He looked Nickel over speculatively, said, "Maybe this winter we'll get a calf, couple pigs, see how we do."

Joe found them fixing a section of fence that had been knocked down by a fallen tree limb. "Don't let him turn you into a farmer," he warned. "Too hard a life."

"He's right," Pop said, but he kept right on teaching Nickel about the farm. And Nickel kept right on learning.

Chapter 7

Nickel started hearing talk about something called Field Day, asked Logan what it was.

Logan said, "It's sports. A whole day of sports. Everybody gets to be on some team, soccer, volleyball, softball. There's other stuff, too. It's fun."

"Some fun," Tyler said glumly, but when the other boys laughed, he did, too. Tyler still hadn't found the sport he was good at.

"There'll be sign-up sheets tomorrow," Logan said. "You choose what you want to play."

At supper Nickel told Joe about it.

"They used to have that at the old school," Joe said. "Used to be fun."

"I'm going to sign up for soccer," Nickel said.

"Whatever you do, you'll be champ," Starla said matter-of-factly.

When Nickel got to school next morning, the sign-up sheets were posted on the wall. Big crowd around them. He decided to wait until lunchtime.

Logan and Tyler went along. Logan had already signed up. "You should have done it this morning, if you want soccer," he said. "The sheets get filled up fast."

Nickel hadn't known it worked that way, hoped there was still space, was glad to see there was.

Tyler hadn't signed up at all. "I always try to get out of it," he said. "Once I did."

Nickel thought it would be awful not to be good at sports. To Tyler it was just an inconvenience, not important, but, since sports were important to the school, he had to go along.

Robbo's name headed the soccer sheet.

"What did he do? Sleep outside the door so he'd be first?" Nickel asked. Added his name to the bottom of the list. Looked up to see that he'd made that crack at the wrong time.

Robbo pushed in front of him. "That's what you should have done," he said, "because, unfortunately, all the slots were filled before you signed up." He whipped out a pencil and slashed across Nickel's name, ripping the paper.

There'd been a time, not long ago, when Nickel would have dived right in. Fought with Robbo, whether he could win or not. But it would bring on too much trouble. That part hadn't mattered much before. Everybody around him had been in trouble, too. But he was in a good place now. He didn't want to louse it up.

So he gave Robbo the hardest look he could put

on and turned away. Robbo hadn't changed Nickel's mind about playing. But he would sign up when Robbo wasn't around.

He did, too, but when he checked it out later, his name was gone again, and another name was in its place. He signed up once more, but he knew that it wouldn't stay. Robbo or one of his sneaky little friends would take care of that. They did. Nickel didn't bother to sign up anymore.

In gym Mr. Highfield told them the soccer sheet was filled. "We're going to have two killer teams," he said. Forever enthusiastic. It made you laugh. But it also made you enthusiastic.

He stopped Nickel as they were leaving the field. "I thought you'd sign up," he said. "You're a good player."

Robbo slowed down. Listened.

"I did," Nickel said. "It got crossed off."

Mr. Highfield didn't look too surprised. Maybe he'd noticed the rip in the paper. Seen the name under the scribble. "Well, you're in," he said.

"Thanks," Nickel said. Didn't look at Robbo's face. Didn't have to.

This time the bike wasn't damaged. The tires weren't slit. At least not that you could see. Because the bike wasn't there at all. When Nickel walked out of the school to ride home, there was nothing to ride. Robbo and the rest were watching him, laughing. He tried not to let them see they'd made him feel bad.

He wished Tyler or Logan were there, but they lived in town, took the bus to school. There was nothing to do but walk home, so that's what he started to do. He hadn't gotten far when he heard somebody running to catch up with him. He glanced over his shoulder, saw Justin, Robbo's best friend or main slave, depending on how you looked at it. Nickel kept walking, didn't say anything.

"Where's your bike?" Justin asked, pretend friendly.

"You tell me," Nickel said.

"How would I know?" Justin asked.

Nickel didn't answer. He was concentrating on not stopping and punching Justin in the mouth. His shoulders tensed, his arms got rigid. His hands went into fists, just on their own, without him thinking about it.

Maybe Justin saw him tightening up. He started talking faster. "I've heard that some of the guys are mad at you."

He waited. Nickel didn't comment, just walked faster. Justin had shorter legs, had to scurry along to stay beside him.

"They say you're a show-off," he panted. "You think you're such a great soccer player. And you laugh at everybody else."

It was hard not to say anything to that, but Nickel kept walking.

"And then you got Mr. Highfield to let you play on the soccer team on Field Day," he said. "You think you're too good to sign up like the rest of us."

Nickel didn't want to talk to this guy. Couldn't help himself. "So what?" he said.

Justin seemed glad for any reaction. "That's not fair," he said.

If Nickel hadn't been so mad, he might have laughed. As if fairness had anything to do with this. "So what?" he said.

"The guys think you should drop out," Justin said. "With you on, there're too many players. Some of us won't be able to play the whole game."

"So what?" Nickel said. Then he couldn't stand any more of it. "Get away from me," he told Justin.

Justin kept on talking. "We think you should tell Mr. Highfield—"

Nickel swung toward him, gave him a hard push. Turned away, walking fast. Didn't even watch to see if he fell, or if he was coming after him. He was shaking all over with anger, almost hoping that Justin would chase after him, jump him, so that Nickel could pound his face in.

He kept walking, never turned, and nothing happened. He reached the old farm road and knew by then that nothing was going to happen. When he reached the lane leading home, he turned and looked back. An empty road, trees on either side bright with red and yellow leaves, a squirrel chattering angrily.

Nickel's shakes eased off. His anger cooled as he turned into the lane that led to the farmhouse. He felt safe here. He had never had a place where he felt so safe.

He wasn't thinking about Cougar, not even when he saw some of the cats, backs arched, tails fluffed out, staring at something behind the stone wall of the ruined barn. As he approached, they looked at him wildly and took off. Then he saw the horse. Just standing there. Cougar.

Nickel didn't know anything about horses, but he could understand why Joe had been so proud of this one. He looked solid as a rock; his coat gleamed in the sunlight. Nickel walked closer. Cautiously. Didn't want to scare him off. The horse dipped his head, shook it, stood his ground.

Nickel stopped walking and just looked. He had never had more than glimpses before. The horse looked back, his large brown eyes staring deeply into Nickel's. Unexpectedly, Nickel felt sorry. From a distance the horse seemed proud, almost fierce. But up close Nickel saw sadness. Loneliness. It hurt Nickel to look at him.

Slowly he raised his arm, reached out his hand toward the animal. "Hey, Cougar," he said softly.

The horse's ears went up, his nostrils quivered. A hoof stamped silently against the ground.

Nickel eased closer. "Come on, Cougar," he whispered.

The horse hesitated, then slowly stretched his neck, leaning toward Nickel. Nickel stood still, hand out, waiting for the touch of Cougar's nose.

"Where's your bike?"

Nickel jumped, flashed a look back at Joe, only a split second, but when he turned back, Cougar was gone.

Gone! Cougar had been right there, right in front of him, his head just inches away from Nickel's hand. In another instant they would have touched, he would have run his hand down Cougar's bony face, felt the warm breath from his velvety nose.

Or would he? Was there warmth and breath to feel? Was there anything? Would he really have touched the animal? Or would his arm have passed through some cold, misty nothing?

And where was Cougar now? Nickel tried to imagine his disappearance. Was it quick? Gradual? Did he just fade out, or did he vanish instantly, like a soap bubble popping?

Was he really gone? Or was he still there, watching Nickel with lonely eyes?

A hand on his shoulder made him jump. "You okay?" Joe asked.

"Yeah," Nickel said vaguely. It was hard to tear his thoughts away from Cougar. He almost told Joe what had happened, but something held him back. Cougar had been Joe's horse, but Joe couldn't see him. It must really be like Pop said. Cougar was Nickel's horse now.

Nickel didn't understand it. But he couldn't tell Joe.

"Where's your bike?" Joe asked again.

"Gone," Nickel said.

"Gone? What do you mean, gone?"

"Stolen." Nickel walked away. He didn't want to hear Joe blow up.

But Joe followed him. "What's going on at that school? Do I have to go over there and break somebody's neck?"

Nickel went into the house, Joe right behind him, still making threats. Joe's mother was in the kitchen. She always was when Nickel got home from school, with a snack set out on the table for him. "What's the ruckus?" she asked.

"Somebody stole Nickel's bike," Joe said. Made it sound like it was Nickel's fault.

Mom put an arm around Nickel, pulled him close. "Don't you care, sweetheart," she said. "We'll get you a better bike." She gave him a squeeze and steered him to the table. "Look what I made for you," she said. "Apple crisp."

Joe was still storming. "What good is getting another bike? They'll just steal that, too. I'll have to go over there, straighten somebody out."

Mom put another dish on the table. "Here, Josiah, apple crisp, it's still warm."

Nickel looked up, smiled. "It's awful good, Joe."

Joe sighed. He wasn't finished yelling. But he couldn't resist the apple crisp.

* * *

Joe must have talked things over with Starla; they must have decided something had to be done about the bike. They came out to where Nickel and Mom were working at the kitchen table. Mom was the one who helped Nickel with his homework when he needed it. Which was often. He'd never done very well in school. He'd never even tried, so he'd missed a lot.

Mom loved helping. Said she'd always liked learning. "I was smart as a whip in school," she bragged. "Even thought about college. But I decided I'd rather marry Lindale."

"Couldn't you have done both?" Nickel asked when she said that.

"Didn't want to do both," Mom said.

Now Nickel was finishing up the last of the apple crisp while Mom talked about his history chapter. It always made more sense after she explained it. Then Joe and Starla came out and started questioning Nickel about the bike. Who slashed the tires? Who stole it? Was this the way things went at this school?

"It's just guys joking around," Nickel said. He tried to make it seem unimportant. But his throat tightened. It was hard to say anything.

He did want his bike back. He didn't like the idea of Robbo and his gang getting away with pushing him around. But he didn't have any real proof that Robbo was behind it. And even if he did, what good would that do? They'd just have Robbo in for counseling. Nickel, too. They might look into Nickel's past records. Find out he hadn't been an angel. Probably decide it was his fault as much as Robbo's. Nickel had been through enough of that stuff. He didn't want adults in this thing. No school authorities, no family members.

But he didn't know how to explain. So he insisted, "It's a joke," and Joe and Starla gave it up. For the time anyway.

Chapter 8

Tyler still hadn't signed up for Field Day. "Maybe nobody will notice until it's too late," he said hopefully.

Logan burst out laughing. Wouldn't say why. Tyler got suspicious, ran for the sign-up sheets, but they'd been taken down.

"You did it again, didn't you!" he shouted at Logan. "You signed me up for something."

"Congratulations," Logan said. "You're on the soccer team."

Tyler's expression made Logan and Nickel laugh so hard, they had to hang on to the wall to keep from falling down. Tyler tried to be mad, ended up laughing along with them.

"You were going to have to play something," Logan said. "I just made up your mind for you."

"I hope I get assigned to your team," Tyler said. "I'll make sure everybody knows why I'm there losing the game for them."

Nickel told them about his bike, and Logan and Tyler were almost as mad as Joe had been about it.

The difference was that they knew who was behind it, knew that accusing him wouldn't solve anything and wouldn't get the bike back, either. They didn't have any answers or even any sensible suggestions about what to do, but they were on Nickel's side, and that made him feel good.

But when they went outside for soccer and Nickel saw Robbo standing there smiling like the cat that swallowed the canary, the good feeling went away. All he felt was anger. This guy thought he could get away with slashing tires, stealing bikes, pushing kids around. Not only thought he could; he really did get away with it.

But there was one thing he couldn't do, no matter how much he wanted to, no matter how much he tried. Even with the help of his stupid little friends, he couldn't play soccer better than Nickel.

That day Nickel made sure Robbo knew it. Made him face the fact. Pushed his nose in it and rubbed. His anger did it, made him play harder, rougher, faster. Everybody was watching him; they'd never seen him like that, not laughing, not playing for fun, playing only to win. When class was over, he walked off the field as if he were alone in the world, not seeing anyone, not hearing, until his anger ran out of him with his sweat.

In the cafeteria Tyler and Logan couldn't stop talking about it.

"You didn't need anybody else on your team," Tyler said.

"I wanted to watch you," Logan said, "but it was too much fun watching Robbo. His eyes kept getting bigger and bigger and his face got purpler and purpler. I kept waiting for the explosion."

"He ran close to me once," Tyler said. "He was, like, growling."

"There was no way I was going to get close to that guy," Logan said. "I didn't want to be nearby when he burst."

They all snickered, glanced over at Robbo. He was watching them. Nickel looked away quickly, tried not to laugh, snorted into his sandwich. That made Tyler choke on his juice, and that set Logan off. The three of them laughed helplessly. Knew they were making Robbo madder than ever, which made them laugh even more.

"I'm glad I ride the bus," Logan said when they finally got control of themselves. "Watch yourself after school, Nickel."

"I will," Nickel said. "Get serious, guys. He knows we're laughing at him."

But Tyler snickered out loud and that broke up Nickel and Logan again. They left the cafeteria, still laughing.

It didn't seem quite so funny when school was out and Nickel was on his way home. He walked through the development, aware that Robbo, Justin, and a kid called Dodger were following him.

He tried to tell himself they weren't, that any minute they'd split up and head for their own homes. It was a dark day, getting ready to rain, not a day to hang around outside.

But when he reached the old road and turned to look, they were still coming, riding slowly in arcs to keep from losing their balance, each arc bringing them a little closer to Nickel. He walked faster, but as they left the development, the space between them narrowed even more. Nickel wanted to run, wouldn't let himself. They were trying to scare him. He wasn't going to let them know it was working.

They kept coming, got close. Nickel spun around and faced them, wishing now that he had run while he had the chance. The guys dropped their bikes, closed in, surrounded him. Robbo suddenly reached out and gave him a push. Almost at once Justin pushed him from the other side, then Dodger from the back. Nickel staggered, just managed to stay upright. Robbo pushed him again, so did the other guys, and Nickel tried to strike out, couldn't get his balance, was knocked from side to side. They started hitting him and he tried to fight, tried to get away and run, but there were three of them and not much he could do. Once in a while his fist connected with someone, but much more often he was the one who was hit. Then he was on the ground, dizzy, not trying to fight anymore, just trying to protect his head. He heard the boys go away. No one had said a word.

Nickel sat up, stayed there for a while, arms on his knees, head on his arms. He felt sick to his stomach. Didn't feel mad yet, didn't even hurt yet. Just dazed, unbelieving.

It was the rain that finally made him get up. It pattered on the dry, brittle leaves, then, as he reached the farm lane, became a downpour. He ran, his feet slipping sideways into the ruts, reached the burned-out barn, stopped, not sure what to do.

He saw a puff of smoke come from the side of the barn, heard voices. Joe and Pop, watching the rain. He didn't want them to see him, didn't want them to know he'd been in a fight.

He had to go inside, get it over with, count on Mom not noticing anything.

She did, though. Right away. "You been fighting?" she asked.

"I fell down," Nickel said.

There was a cupcake on the table and a glass of milk. Nickel sat down, took a bite of cupcake. It was like a wad of cotton in his mouth. He forced it down with the help of the milk. Knew Mom was watching him, but he couldn't eat any more. Finally looked up, into her worried eyes, and knew he was going to cry.

He pushed away from the table, caught the chair before it went over backward, went for the door to the upstairs. Mom stood in his way. "What's wrong?"

He faced her, tried to say, "Nothing," but his lips quivered too much. He knew that if he tried to talk, he would just blubber. There was stamping on the back steps, Pop and Joe coming in.

"Come on," Mom said. Grabbed his arm, pushed him up the stairs. By the time they reached the upstairs hall, he was crying like a baby. Mom shoved him into the bathroom, started the water running in the tub. "Get those clothes off," she said.

Nickel grabbed a tissue, wiped at his running eyes and nose, hating himself.

"Undress, Nickel," Mom said.

"When you leave," he mumbled.

"Don't be silly," Mom said. "I need to see how bad hurt you are."

"I'm not bad hurt," Nickel said, and stood there.

"I raised one boy," Mom said. "I don't expect you have anything that would surprise me." When he still hesitated, she snorted impatiently. "Leave your undies on, if you're so modest."

Miserable as he was, the word *undies* struck Nickel funny. With a choked laugh, he started to undress.

His clothes showed him how Mom had known he'd been fighting. One sleeve almost ripped from his jacket, bloodstains on both knees of his jeans, and, over everything, dirt that had turned to mud from the rain.

"Not as bad as I feared. Scratches. You'll have some bruises." Mom looked at him hard. "Who hit you?"

"Nobody." Nickel wanted to say more, convince her to forget it, but he couldn't do it. Just stood there shivering.

"You're cold. Get in that nice hot water," Mom said.

Nickel stepped into the big, old tub, sank down into the foam from the bubble bath Mom had added. He let himself slide all the way under, pushed himself back up, sank back down to his chin.

"Now you can take off your undies." Mom gathered up his ruined clothes and left the room. Nickel felt a tickle of laughter. He'd forgotten about his undies.

He stayed in the tub for a long time, even though it was the only bathroom in the house. Nobody bothered him. He wondered if that meant Mom had told them. He hoped she hadn't. Joe and Starla would be up to school, screaming, adding to the trouble. Other people would get involved, maybe decide that Joe and Starla were too young to raise Nickel, or that Mom and Pop couldn't control him. His real mother might even get brought into it. That would be bad. He never wanted to get mixed up in that kind of life again.

Nickel liked it here. He liked having a snack waiting when he got home, he liked talking about farm things with Pop and watching TV with him, he even half liked the homework sessions at the kitchen table. He knew a lot of kids would think it was dull. Joe had when he was a kid. Still did. But it suited

Nickel. He wanted to stay. If things were going to be bad at school, they would just have to be bad. School wasn't his whole life.

There was pounding on the door. "Did you die in there?" Joe yelled.

"Be right out." Nickel pulled the plug, climbed out of the tub, pushed past Joe, scooted for his room. He jumped into bed, still wet, wrapped up in the covers, heard Joe shout, "Looks like somebody washed a pig in this tub." Smiled, felt himself warming up, shut his eyes, slid into sleep.

Chapter 9

The next day was still kind of rainy, off and on. Pop offered to drive Nickel to school, but Nickel turned him down, afraid he might ask about the fight. Nickel didn't know what to say, didn't know how much he wanted to tell. But maybe Mom hadn't said anything. Seemed like there would have been fireworks if she had, but last night nobody had mentioned it. Nickel had slept through supper. When he'd showed up in the kitchen, Mom had fed him, made him bring his homework out to the table. He'd thought they might skip it for once, but Mom made him work as hard as if he hadn't been crying in the bathtub just a little while ago.

It was getting time for school to start. Nickel tried to hurry, but his thoughts kept slowing him down. He would speed up, then find himself dragging again, eyes on the road, seeing nothing.

He couldn't decide what to do. If it was just him and Robbo, he could handle it. Robbo was big, but Nickel knew how to take care of himself. But it wasn't just the two of them. Robbo had his little gang of attack dogs. Nickel had only himself.

There were probably other guys who had something against Robbo. They just needed to be organized. Nickel knew how that stuff worked. But he didn't want to be part of a gang, didn't want to spend all his time thinking about kids he didn't like. He just wanted to play sports, have friends who made him laugh, learn a little bit in school, have a family that looked out for him. Mom and Pop, that's who he wanted. And they wanted him, too, he knew that. They liked him. They didn't care if he was dumb in school or sloppy around the house. They didn't get mad when he couldn't find words.

Why did Robbo think he had to do this anyway? Didn't he understand that there would always be a better player coming along? There was always somebody better than everybody. It didn't make the game any less fun.

The fields were wet. Gym class was indoors today. The talk was that the weather was clearing, things would dry out, Field Day would be tomorrow as planned.

Changing in the locker room, Nickel saw the bruises on his legs and suddenly anger slashed through him like a knife. He'd never felt that mad before, so mad that his knees felt weak, his vision seemed to blur. When everybody went into the gym, Nickel stayed where he was, sat with his fingers gripping the edge of the bench, fighting down the rage that made him want to get Robbo back, really hurt him.

They were going to spoil things for him. Robbo was. Not the other guys. They didn't plan, they just did whatever Robbo said. They were probably more scared of Robbo than Nickel was.

Logan stuck his head in the door, said, "Mr. Highfield is looking for you," saw Nickel's face. "Are you sick?"

"Yeah." Nickel got up, went into the gym. They were doing drills, Mr. Highfield shouting encouragingly, enthusiastically, preparing them mentally for the big day tomorrow. Nickel went through the motions, but his heart wasn't in it. He felt jumpy, his timing was way off.

"You okay, Nick?" Mr. Highfield asked, and Nickel said, "I'm okay."

"I hope you're more okay than this tomorrow." Laughing, not really worried. Nickel couldn't laugh back. He didn't know what he'd be like tomorrow.

Logan and Tyler saw that something was wrong, probably suspected what had happened, but Nickel couldn't tell them yet. He was still too mad to talk about it.

At the end of the day he walked out of the building and just stood there, not knowing what to expect, not sure he wanted to take a chance getting jumped again. A girl, Lisa, was there. She smiled at him sometimes, but Nickel wasn't comfortable around girls, usually said something stupid, so he didn't smile back. But he didn't feel so shy when he had other things on his mind. She started talking to him about Field Day, wanted to know what team he would be on.

"You weren't on the sign-up sheets," she said. Nickel was surprised. She had looked for his name. He told her it kept getting erased. She nodded, said, "Robbo," surprising him again. "You're the boy with the ghost horse," she said.

Nickel didn't know what to say. He hadn't expected Logan and Tyler to tell the whole school about Cougar.

Lisa waited, then said, "What's it like having a ghost horse? Do you ride it?"

"It's not like that," Nickel said. "It's not a pet."

"Well, what *is* it like?" Lisa persisted. Nickel wanted to talk to her, but he couldn't concentrate. Justin had come from somewhere, was watching them. I'm probably talking to Robbo's girl, Nickel thought. Justin's probably taking notes.

A car drove up and Lisa said, "Good luck tomorrow," ran and got in. She waved from the window, and Nickel waved back. Watched the car drive away, past the few bikes remaining in the parking lot. One of the bikes caught his attention. It was his.

Nickel stared, walked over for a closer look. It

really was his bike. He hadn't even looked for it, hadn't expected ever to see it again. He looked around. No sign of Justin now, but he was probably the one who had put the bike here, brought it from wherever they had stashed it.

He looked for damage, but it seemed okay, so he got on, started riding slowly home. Through the development, quiet now, most of the kids inside staring at TVs and computer screens. Down the old road, edged in dying weeds, slippery with wet fallen leaves. Nobody followed him, and now Nickel understood that they wouldn't. From the way he'd played today, they thought they'd scared him into a deal.

He rode past the place where he'd been jumped yesterday, and anger shot through him, anger at what Robbo had done, anger that stupid kids like that could have the upper hand. The guys would leave him alone now. He could even have his bike back. As long as he did what they wanted. They must be feeling pretty good about themselves. They'd settled the problem of Nickel.

But maybe they were wrong. Nickel didn't know himself whether they were or not. He wondered how many other kids Robbo had pushed around, scared into doing things his way. He wondered if Robbo knew that it was possible to push people too far, farther than they could take. Make them *too* scared, so that they looked for a way to protect themselves, became more dangerous than the one they were afraid of.

Nickel didn't want to be pushed that far.

As he bumped and rattled up the lane, Pop stepped out from the rubble of the barn. "Got your bike back," he said.

Nickel leaned the bike against the barn wall. "It showed up in the parking lot."

Pop took a long drag on his cigarette, coughed the smoke back out. "I hear you had a little trouble yesterday."

Nickel was glad he knew, glad he hadn't had to tell him himself. "It's because I'm good at soccer," he said. "Somebody wants me to not be so good."

Pop nodded. Nickel felt like he wanted more of a reaction. He didn't want Pop going up to school or anything, but he wanted something, advice maybe. But, after all, what good was advice? No matter what Nickel did, he was going to be the loser.

"They think they've convinced me," he said. "That's why they gave me back my bike."

"Have they convinced you?"

Nickel frowned, looked away. "I don't know."

As he went into the house, he remembered that he hadn't looked for Cougar. He'd taken to keeping an eye out, checking the bushes along the lane, the field of corn stubble on one side, the weedy field on the other. Today all he had thought about was Robbo. If Cougar had been there, Nickel would never have known. One more thing to hold against Robbo.

Chapter 10

On Field Day the sun was shining. Pop came outside when Nickel left for school. Nickel knew he was worrying about him, thinking about what he might be in for today, but he didn't say anything, just watched Nickel get on his bike and start off down the lane. Nickel took a quick glance back, waved a quick wave. He had to watch what he was doing, keep the wheels out of ruts, avoid protruding roots.

Then, not fifteen feet ahead, the horse flashed like a black flame across the lane, leaped like wildfire across the cornfield fence. Sparks flew from his coat in the early morning sunlight.

Nickel jumped from his bike and let it go, pushed through honeysuckle to the fence, climbed it, and jumped down into the field. "Cougar." Hardly more than a gasp, but the horse stopped, turned, looked full into Nickel's face. Nickel held out his hand, waited, hoping this time they would touch. Cougar pranced nervously in place, neck arched like a circus horse, then suddenly reared and galloped away. He raced toward the far fence, mane and tail like smoke in the wind. He swerved suddenly, turned back, headed straight for Nickel as if to run him down, but Nickel didn't flinch, never even thought of it, just stood watching as the horse veered, made a circuit of the field, still running full out. There were glints of gold in the black coat. Even the hoofs glittered with gold specks. And those hoofs made no sound. Kicked up no dust. Left no trail.

Nickel watched until all at once, in a blink, he was gazing at an empty field. Corn stubble, stiff and dry, weeds moving in a light breeze. That was all.

He climbed back over the fence, stood there awhile, looking out where the horse had been. Then he turned, picked up his bike, walked it slowly back up the lane. Pop stood there, watching him.

Nickel propped the bike against the barn wall, looked up at Pop. "No use taking it. They'll wreck it."

"So they didn't convince you," Pop said.

"I guess not." Thought he should warn Pop. "There might be trouble." He hesitated. "Maybe more than you want to put up with."

Pop looked away, toward the house, back at Nickel. "I drove one boy away," he said. "I'm not about to do it again."

A rush of feelings Nickel had never felt before swirled around in his chest, choked his throat, burned his eyes. He didn't try for words. He wouldn't be able to get them out anyway. So he took a deep, shaky breath, said, "I just saw Cougar."

"I saw you looking." Pop gave him a push. "Get going. You're late."

Nickel wondered if all Field Days at all schools were like this. It was so loose, so disorganized. So much fun.

There was a softball game first thing, hilarious to watch. Mr. Highfield must have sat up all night with his sign-up sheets, deciding who would play where, trying to balance the teams evenly. He'd probably done the best he could, but with teams made up of boys and girls from three different grades, every play was a surprise.

"Some of these kids don't even seem to know the rules of the game," Nickel said.

"Doesn't matter," Logan said. "All you have to do to play on Field Day is to sign up and show up."

"Some of us don't even have to sign up," Tyler said.

"Quit complaining," Logan said. "I could have signed you up for this team."

"You should have," Tyler said. "They're not as serious as the soccer guys."

Logan nodded. "He's right. One mistake and those soccer guys will kill him."

"That's right, Tyler," Nickel agreed. "We will."

There were other things to do besides watching the ball game, and they tried them all, shooting baskets, running relay races, and, of course, eating snacks. They stocked up at the snack truck, went back to watch some more of the softball game. It showed signs of going on forever, so Mr. Highfield put an assistant in charge while he assembled the volleyball team. That was a lot easier for him, just a case of dividing the group in half.

Nickel saw the girl who had talked to him in the parking lot. "Is that Robbo's girlfriend?" he asked.

Logan said, "Who? I didn't know he had one."

Nickel pointed her out and both boys turned to him, surprised, grinning. "That's Lisa," Tyler said. "That's my sister."

Nickel looked at Tyler, at Logan, back at Tyler. "But she's pretty," he said.

"Why does that surprise you?" Logan asked. "Don't you think Tyler's pretty?"

"Yeah," Tyler said. "Don't you think I'm pretty?" He stretched the corners of his mouth up with his thumbs, pulled his eyelids down with his fingers.

"I didn't before," Nickel said, "but you look much better now."

Lisa was the first server. She ran over to Nickel, giggling, whispered, "This is for you." Then she ran back into position and hit the ball up and out of bounds. She looked back at Nickel and shrugged.

"No coordination," Tyler said. "Runs in the family."

But Nickel hadn't even noticed that she had messed up. He watched the whole game, even after Tyler and Logan left him to shoot some baskets. He'd never played volleyball, but it wasn't hard to follow. Before long he knew the rules, even though he spent a lot of time watching Lisa, who seemed to be breaking them all. She kept saying, "Oops," and "Sorry," but it didn't really seem to bother her.

Nickel thought she might come over to him after the game, but she just waved and went off with a group of girls, so he looked around to see what was next. Some kids were out on the track, but most people were having lunch, either food from the cafeteria or pizza from the truck. Running into Logan and Tyler, their faces smeared with sauce, made him decide on pizza.

"You just get prettier every time I see you," he told Tyler.

"If you like him in pizza, you should see how good he looks in chocolate milk," Logan said, shaking his carton, but at Tyler's expression, he changed his mind, started drinking the milk instead.

"Save your energy for soccer," Nickel said, and a thrill went through him. He wasn't sure if it was a good or a bad feeling. It would be fun to shock Robbo and the other guys who thought they had him scared. That part of the thrill was good. But then what? Was it dangerous to cross Robbo like that? Or had he already done all he dared to do?

The softball game had finally been called a tie, and the track had erupted with relay racers and broad jumpers and sprinters. It looked like total confusion, and maybe it was, but everybody seemed to be having a good time, except possibly some of the teachers.

It was getting time for the soccer game, which was the last scheduled event of the day, and by now Nickel had a better idea of what to expect. This wasn't something serious. Like the softball and volleyball games, there would be a big disparity in playing ability, from very good to first-timers. Strategy was out. This was strictly for fun.

But Robbo had scratched Nickel's name off the sign-up sheet. To him the soccer game must seem important. Nickel started to feel that nervous excitement again. He walked over to the field, saw a bunch of kids warming up for the game, ran out, and joined a circle of players kicking the ball to one another. One of the kids wasn't getting it right, didn't seem to have any idea how to do it. Nickel took him aside, gave him a quick lesson. He didn't expect it to do much good, not for today's game anyway, but the kid was grateful. Nickel liked the idea of being able to teach somebody, help somebody. He thought that must be how Mom felt teaching him.

Mr. Highfield showed up, looking a little frazzled, but still upbeat. He gathered the players around him so he could announce teams and positions. Nickel and Robbo weren't on the same team, as Nickel had expected. They were the best players, and Mr.

Highfield was trying to make the teams as even as possible.

Tyler was assigned to Nickel's team. He started acting up right away, shouting, "I win. I win. With Nickel we can't lose." When Logan was put on the other team, Tyler carried on worse than ever. "Tough break, Logan," he said. "All you can do now is try to be a good sport when we crush you."

The other kids took it as a joke, especially the ones from other classes who didn't know how much Robbo hated to lose. But Robbo wasn't laughing.

The game started out fun. It was almost a free-for-all, since a lot of the kids had never played together before, and nobody knew who to trust with the ball, which kids knew what to do with it and which ones would just stand there and watch it go by. Mr. Highfield had done a good job. The teams were pretty evenly matched, except for the goalies. The kid playing on Robbo's team was in a lower grade, but he was good, and the score began to show it.

Nickel watched the goalie, looking for his weaknesses, more from force of habit than anything else. This was only Field Day, no need to play all out the way he usually did.

Then Robbo changed his mind for him. The other team had just scored another goal, and Robbo was running back into position. As he passed Tyler he bumped him hard, knocked him sideways, spit out the words, "Looks like you were wrong, big mouth."

And he sent Nickel a nasty grin.

It was the grin that did it. Plainer than words, it showed what Robbo felt, that Nickel was no longer a problem, that he was too scared to cross Robbo anymore. But it straightened out Nickel's thinking. He knew that Robbo was wrong.

Suddenly Nickel was grinning, too, as excitement and anticipation filled his body with so much energy that he couldn't stand still. By the time this game was over, Robbo would understand that there were some things he couldn't control, no matter how much he wanted to, no matter what he did.

There was no use playing to win; the team just didn't have it. They were too far behind now anyway. So instead of playing against the other team, Nickel played against Robbo. Wherever Robbo went, Nickel was right behind him, or beside him, or in front of him. And it drove Robbo crazy.

That was the only explanation for what happened. Robbo couldn't stand being stalked. At first he just looked surprised and then annoyed when everywhere he turned brought him face to face with Nickel. He tried threats, but Nickel just laughed in his face. He kicked at Nickel, and Nickel danced away and then closed in on him again. It didn't matter if Robbo had the ball or not, Nickel was right there anyway, standing shoulder to shoulder with him, or breathing down his neck and laughing.

All at once, Robbo seemed to break. He began to

yell curses at Nickel, then started swinging at him, and not just at *him*. Everybody in range came under attack, and the last half of the game was more a series of time-outs for fouls than anything else. Both sides watched unbelievingly as the penalty kicks added up to a win for Nickel's team.

Chapter 11

The kid Nickel had coached, who'd turned out to be on his team, invited the team to his house for a victory celebration. Probably the first time he'd been on a winning team in his life.

There weren't a lot of kids. The boy lived in the development near the school, so the bus kids couldn't come, but it was on Nickel's way home, so he stopped in.

It was a bigger deal than he had expected. A lot of food. Victory or defeat, this kid had planned to have a celebration, no matter what. Lyle, his name was. The party was in his basement, which was like an arcade, but better because everything was free. Besides the usual video games, there was a Ping-Pong table and a small pool table. Nickel was fascinated. He'd never known anybody with so much stuff.

"If I lived here, I'd never go outside again," he said. He never touched the food—the games kept him too busy—but most of the other kids had been here before, were more interested in eating and talking about the game.

"You should have invited Robbo," one of them said. "He won it for us." Everybody laughed. Nickel heard them talking, but he didn't join in. He didn't feel like they'd won anything.

The other kids did, though, and they gave Nickel all the credit. Not because he had played well, just because they figured he had pushed Robbo over the edge, driven him into handing them the game.

Nickel was enjoying Lyle's basement arcade more than he had enjoyed the soccer. He went from game to game, tried out the pool table, was into a game of Ping-Pong with Lyle when he realized the last of the kids were leaving.

"Is it late?" he asked. "I guess I ought to go home."

"Just finish this game," Lyle urged. So he did. And then another one. When he finally stepped outside the house he was surprised to see that it was dark. He'd been at Lyle's a lot longer than he'd thought.

He walked quickly, hoping nobody at home would be worried or mad, looking forward to supper. He hadn't eaten since the pizza at lunch. Too bad about all that good stuff at Lyle's, but the games had just been too much fun.

He tried not to think about how dark it was, how alone he was, and how dumb he'd been to turn down Lyle's mother's offer of a ride home, tonight of all nights.

Nickel had left the development, was walking down the old road, when a little ahead of him, just beyond the ditch on the right-hand side of the road, the tall, dry weeds shook, just for a second. Some animal probably, trying to hide. But even while he told himself that, he knew it wasn't an animal, realized, with a jolt of terror, that he was in danger.

He was running before he knew it, fought his way through the weeds and bushes on the opposite side of the road, and cut through the cornfield where Cougar had run that morning. He heard footsteps pounding behind him, but he didn't look, just put all his concentration into getting away. His fear gave him an edge, gave him more speed than whoever was following him.

Nickel headed for the fence that edged the farm lane, found the place where Cougar had leaped into the cornfield that morning. It was the easiest way through the fencerow, just some honeysuckle to get through, but whoever was following him wouldn't know that. With any luck they would be slowed down by brambles and vines long enough to give Nickel a chance to get home.

He crawled between the fence rails, fought through the weeds, raced up the lane toward the farmhouse. Then at the last second his pride got in the way. He couldn't do it, couldn't run to Mom and Pop for protection. He had to get out of this by himself.

So instead of running up the porch steps to safety, Nickel ran down into the barnyard. It was big, dark, cluttered with trash from the fire. A good place to hide. He pressed himself against the inside wall, breathing hard, listening. Heard movement on the floor above. Had a sudden pleasing picture of them all falling through the hole and breaking their necks. But no one fell. He heard sharp whispers, movement, then silence, long enough for him to hope they'd given up, gone away.

Then he heard footsteps on the other side of the wall. Suddenly the barnyard didn't seem like such a good hiding place after all. Nickel decided he had to get out, wondered if he had time to run across, out the other side, into the field before they saw him, or at least before they could get him. Maybe he could circle around, make it back to the house, where he should have gone in the first place.

He crouched low, meaning to take off running, but instead he tripped, fell hard on his knees. He couldn't believe it. Something was tangled around his ankle, holding him in place. He reached around, felt metal, ripped it away. But he had missed his chance to run. He threw himself flat where he was, pushed his body into the soft dirt, tried to become invisible, tried to remain perfectly still.

But it was hard to lie still. There was something in the ground where he was lying, more of the metal that had caught his ankle probably, and it was poking into his chest, sticking into his thigh. Then he heard someone stumbling toward him, and he forgot about the pain. They came close to him, too close. Nickel had tensed himself to spring to his feet, ready to fight, when he felt a lurch from somewhere beneath him, heard a string of swear words, recognized Justin's voice yelling, "I'm cut!"

"Quiet!" That was Robbo.

Justin's voice came from farther away, outside the barnyard. "Look at that. Blood. I'll probably get lockjaw."

That sounded all right to Nickel. Justin was almost whining now. "It was a piece of metal. It whipped out of the ground and cut me."

"Will you shut up?" Robbo said.

Then a light, Pop's voice, "Who's out there?" and Nickel heard the thud of running feet. It was quiet for a few minutes, and Nickel knew Pop must be standing there looking, listening, wondering what was going on, where Nickel was. After a while the door closed, but the light stayed on. Nickel knew he should go in, let them know he was okay, stop their worry. But he couldn't yet.

He'd gotten away this time. But what about tomorrow? The next day? Anger, fear, a sense of helplessness filled him, nauseated him.

As he lay there in the dirt, he realized that whatever had been poking him wasn't poking anymore. It almost seemed to have changed position, adjusted under his body. He started to get up, pushed himself off the ground, and his hand touched something warm. The unexpectedness of it brought him to his feet fast. Warmth meant something alive, something living under there, a possum maybe, or a rat. Something. All at once Nickel was scared. He couldn't get out of the barnyard fast enough, kept looking over his shoulder as if something might be following him. Looked back and saw that his hiding place had been on Cougar's grave.

Later Nickel stood at his bedroom window, looking out at the barn, wondering what had happened to him in there. After the guys had run away and he was safe, why did he get so scared? It wasn't like he'd never been alone in the dark before.

The thing was, he hadn't felt completely alone. He felt a little tingle of fear again, remembering, and when a shadow beside the barn wall moved, his heart seemed to jump into his throat, but it was just one of the cats, stalking something, as usual. The cats spent their nights hunting, leaving little mouse bodies at the door for the family to step on in the morning.

He'd gotten off easy with Mom and Pop. They were a little mad because he hadn't let them know he'd be late, especially since Pop knew there might be trouble over the game. It didn't occur to Nickel to explain that he wasn't used to calling home. Until he went to stay with Joe and Starla, *he* had been the one wondering where everybody was.

Mom had heated up his supper, and while he ate

they got the whole story out of him, at least the part about being chased and hiding in the barn. Well, that really *was* the whole story. The part about being scared was just his imagination.

Tomorrow was Saturday, no school, he could stay up as late as he wanted. The house was quiet. Joe and Starla were out someplace, Mom was murmuring and laughing on the phone. Nickel went downstairs to watch TV with Pop.

Chapter 12

All through the night, dreams disturbed Nickel, waking him and then evaporating when he tried to remember them. He was finally deep in sleep when he was jolted awake by a noise from outside. A loud noise, he thought. The walls still seemed to be ringing with it as he came to. He lay listening, but it didn't come again, and now he wasn't sure if there had really been a sound or if it was just another dream.

He got out of bed, went to the window, and saw that it was close to morning. He watched as trees, vehicles, outbuildings became shapes instead of shadows. His ears were still full of the sound that might not have happened.

He noticed that the cats were gathered around the barn door. One of them must have made an interesting kill. The barn looked mysterious in the morning mist, like a picture of an ancient ruin, an old castle maybe, or a church. Nickel felt an urge to run down there, to go inside, look at the place where he had hidden last night. See if that scary sensation came back. But it was too early; it would still be dark inside the barn. He got into bed to wait for sunrise, surprised himself by sleeping until full daylight.

After breakfast he went out to the barnyard and it wasn't scary at all, just tumbled rocks and charred logs and smoky smell. He walked over to the mound, Cougar's burial mound, wondered how Justin could have missed seeing him there, then remembered with a smile that Justin had been too busy carrying on about lockjaw. From a piece of metal, he said. Nickel had been tangled up in metal last night, too, but he hadn't been cut.

In the daylight he could see the metal clearly, and he realized suddenly that he was looking at a half-buried bicycle. He could see part of a tire sticking out of the ground, the tip of a handlebar. No wonder he'd been uncomfortable lying there, at least until the bicycle had shifted. But it couldn't have shifted by itself. Maybe there *was* something living under there. Maybe Justin had been bitten, not cut, maybe he'd found toothmarks in his leg when he got home last night.

Nickel reached down, pushed away enough dirt to find the handlebars and get a grip, pulled as hard as he could, nearly fell over backward as the bicycle came loose.

He felt a quiver in his hands as they held on to the handlebars, felt it run up his arms—a strange sensation that almost made him drop the bike. He tried to wheel it out into the sunlight where he could see it better, but the tires were shot and the going was so rough that he ended up carrying it in his arms. He could feel the warmth of the bicycle through his shirt.

Mom came outside with food for the cats, which Nickel couldn't see that they needed. If they weren't hungry enough to finish off the things they spent all their time slaughtering, why give them more? They were always ready, though, came running with their tails straight up in the air and dove right in.

He carried the bike over to her, put it down, and held it by the handlebars.

"Well, look at that," Mom said. "You found Josiah's bicycle." She took in the flat tires, bent handlebars, twisted pedals. "I don't think it's worth keeping, do you?"

Nickel felt the shivery feeling, couldn't tell if it came from him or the bike. "I'll ask Joe," he said. But he knew he was going to keep it.

Joe didn't want the bike. He and Pop looked it over, pointed out the damage to Nickel, advised him to junk it. Nickel asked them to help him fix it up.

Joe and Pop both looked doubtful, but they checked out the bike again, examined every element of it, got interested, as Nickel had known they would. They both liked doing stuff like that, tinkering,

Mom called it. She considered it a waste of time, an excuse to stand around talking and smoking. Well, not smoking anymore. Pop swore he'd quit, and so far she'd never caught him at it.

They argued with each other about what could be repaired and what would have to be replaced. The work that could be done without tools, they took care of right then. Nickel was excited. "Look how good it looks already," he said, and Joe said, "Are you kidding?" They all climbed into the truck, ran down to where Joe worked, picked up what they needed to finish the job.

Back home, they went right at it, Nickel watching, in the way, learning. Joe and Pop cussed each other, cussed the bike, disagreed about everything except that it wasn't worth the trouble.

"The frame is bent," Joe said. "The whole bike is out of line. You'll never be able to steer it."

Nickel wasn't worried. He knew they could fix it, and he knew he could ride it. He thought of something he had been wondering about. "What kind of metal is that?" he asked. "Why does it feel so warm?"

Both men looked up from their work. "How do you mean, warm?" Pop asked, and Joe said, "This metal's not warm."

Nickel reached over, touched the metal. It was warm. He didn't say any more about it.

* * *

The men spent all weekend, whatever time they could spare, putting the bike back into condition. Mom thought it was pointless. "You'd be better to get a new bike than try to repair that old wreck," she said.

But Starla was on Nickel's side, or on the bike's side. "It's like bringing something back to life," she said, startling Nickel, but a look at her face told him she didn't mean anything special, she was just talking.

Finally the bike was ready for a test run.

"Just try it to the end of the lane and back," Pop said, and Joe said, "If you can *get* it to the end of the lane."

The bike seemed stiff, and Nickel tried to take it easy at first, but it was impossible to go slow on that rough driveway. He kept having to put a foot down to keep from going over. He put on some speed, and that's when he saw what Joe meant about the steering. If Nickel aimed the handlebars directly ahead, the bike veered to the right, so he had to steer to the left, but not too much to the left, or the bike would try to turn completely around. He was all over the lane, but he got to the end. Everything that Pop and Joe did seemed to work, nothing fell off, and the ride back up the lane was less erratic than the ride down had been.

"You guys are geniuses!" he shouted. "It's perfect."

Joe looked at Pop and shrugged. "This is the kid who thinks I need a new car."

Pop said, "It could use a little more work, Nickel.

Tomorrow we'll try to do something about that steering problem."

Nickel put the bike by the barn wall, alongside his old bike. He would let them work on it if they wanted to. But it was fine with him just the way it was.

The next morning when he left the house for school, the bike was leaning against the back steps. He glanced over at the barn. His old bike was still there. But someone had moved this bike to the house.

Nickel didn't intend to ride to school anymore—it wasn't worth the trouble—but as he passed the bike, the pedal was sticking out farther than it seemed, he stumbled over it, and then his shoestring got tangled in the chain, and by the time he got himself straightened out, he had decided to ride Joe's old bike to school. Or the bike had decided. Nickel wasn't sure.

So he took off, wobbling and weaving down the lane, fighting the handlebars that kept wanting to head him off in another direction, forcing the brakes on when the bike seemed ready to run out from under him. Maybe Joe and Pop were right, it could stand a little more tinkering. But it got him to school.

He was early. The town kids were just hopping off their bus. Lisa saw him, walked over, said, "Congratulations. Tyler's been bragging like he won the game himself, but I know it was you."

"No, it was a funny kind of game," Nickel said.

Tyler ran up, called, "Hey, Lisa, this is for you," and threw a ball of paper backward over his head.

Nickel was afraid she'd be mad or embarrassed, but she laughed, said, "This is for you," and punched Tyler on the arm. "He's been doing that to me all weekend," she told Nickel. "Well, it would have been nice if it had worked."

Nickel mumbled, "It was nice anyway," hoped Tyler wouldn't hear. He did, though, squealed, "Oooh, Nickel," in a high voice. Nickel wished he would go away. It was hard enough to talk to Lisa, but with Tyler listening, it was worse.

"Tyler said you thought I was Robbo's girlfriend," she said, making a face.

Nickel wanted to say something, couldn't think of a thing.

"That would be even worse than being Tyler's sister," Lisa said.

"Well, I'm glad you're not," Nickel said. Realized that didn't make sense. "I mean, I'm glad you're Tyler's sister, but I'm glad you don't like Robbo." That didn't sound right, either. "I mean, maybe you like him, I don't know about that, but I'm glad you're not his girl." He was so aware of Tyler taking it all in, knowing that he would report every word to Logan, that he couldn't talk straight. He was relieved when the bell rang, and he could quit standing there trying to think of things to say.

* * *

The bell at the end of the day gave him a different feeling. He wondered how long he could take it, his stomach squeezing up into a ball like a sick squirrel every time he left the school building.

Justin was close to him on the way out the door. Nickel couldn't resist, asked, "How's the lockjaw?" and Justin flinched as if he'd hit him. Nickel passed Robbo, felt him looking, didn't look back. No direct eye contact was probably safer, like with dogs.

He'd already decided that if he was followed, he wouldn't even try to get home. He'd circle back to school, wait them out in the parking lot, even go back inside and call Pop if he had to. Those guys weren't going to get another chance at him if he could help it.

He got on the battered old bike, headed out, heard Robbo call, "Hey, Nick, you raid a junkyard?" heard Justin laugh, and then something happened, somehow the bike went out of control. The handlebars twisted in his hands, the pedals jerked under his feet, and he found himself turned around, heading straight for Robbo. Robbo tried to hold his ground, probably couldn't believe Nickel would really run into him, but at the last second, disbelief on his face, he threw himself out of the way. Nickel was glad he did. Otherwise he and the bike would have smashed him flat.

Nickel steered the bike around Robbo, where he

sat on the ground looking about as mad as it was possible to get, yelled, "Sorry," and took off for home. He really *was* sorry for whatever had caused the bike to act like that. Nickel would never have pulled such a trick purposely. But every time he thought of Robbo's face, he laughed.

Chapter 13

He fought the bike all the way home. It seemed to have its own ideas about where it wanted to go, kept heading toward the side of the road, toward the field, and it was all Nickel could do to keep it going straight. Then the ride up the farm lane was way too fast, he expected to be bounced off any minute, except that somehow they managed to avoid the worst of the ruts. When they finally arrived at the farmhouse, Nickel's knees felt tight, his hands sore.

Pop came rattling up the lane in his truck. "How'd it go?" he asked, and Nickel told him about his steering problem. "I almost ran into a kid," he said, "but I think I'm getting more used to it now." He ran in the house for his snack, left Pop looking over the bike.

"So you rode that old wreck to school," Mom said.

"It was leaning against the steps this morning," Nickel said. "Joe must have put it there for me. Or Pop."

"That man's been worrying about you all day," Mom said. "Well, we both have. But he couldn't stand it, had to go up to school and make sure nobody got after you."

Nickel didn't know how he felt when he heard that. He didn't want anybody worrying about him, thinking he needed protection. Even so, it felt good to have people on his side. Joe was ready to go up to school and fight anytime Nickel said the word. And Pop had gone there today and waited, watching for trouble, looking out for Nickel.

When Joe came home, he banged out a few more dents and said that was it, Nickel was lucky the bike was as good as it was, he would just have to get used to it. He promised to bring home some paint, dark blue. "The bike's black," Nickel said, and Joe said, "No, it's not, it's blue." He looked at it closely, scratched a fender, said, "It does look black." Looked at Nickel. "It was a dark blue bike."

"Maybe the heat from the fire did something," Nickel said. Wasn't sure if that made sense, but Joe ought to know what color his own bike was. Well, it would be blue again when Nickel painted it tomorrow. Pop gave him some rags and sandpaper, and he started cleaning it up, getting rid of the rust, the smudges from the fire, the grease from the repair job. The bike seemed to lean into his hands as he rubbed it down. Nickel felt its warmth and wondered again how it was that Joe and Pop didn't feel it.

When he'd done all he could, he wheeled it over to the barn, propped it up with the kickstand, stood admiring it. Even before the new paint job, it looked good.

Rain spattered the window as Nickel got ready for bed. He heard the wind gusting, thought he should have put the bikes under cover, looked out to see how bad it was, and saw Cougar. The horse was standing by the barn, head high, not minding the wind that rippled his mane, the rain that ran in silver streaks down his flanks.

Nickel turned, ran downstairs, fumbled with the back-door lock, then the porch-door lock. It took forever. Half dressed, barefooted, he ran out into the cold rain, ran to the barn, seeing before he got there that Cougar was gone. Just the bikes were there, his old one leaning against the wall, and Joe's bike, now Nickel's, black as midnight, except where raindrops reflected the porch light, giving the metal a golden glitter.

No sign of Cougar. So why did Nickel feel that he was still around? He tried to see into the dark, but it was raining hard. Cougar was black; even a few yards away he would be invisible. "Cougar," he called, but his lonely voice gave him the creeps and he didn't call again.

Since he was out here, he might as well put the bikes in the barn. A lot of the roof was gone, but there was still some protection from the weather. He wheeled his old bike in with no problem, but when he tried to get Joe's bike through the doorway, it wouldn't go. The pedals caught in the chinks in the stone wall, the wheels stuck in the ground, the handlebars turned at angles that made it impossible to move it forward. The bike seemed bigger tonight, heavier, and Nickel could hardly handle it. He was soaking wet by now, beginning to feel the cold, so he gave up, left the bicycle outside and went back to his room, leaving a trail of wet leaves behind him.

Chapter 14

The morning was bright, water drops glittering in the sunlight. When he left the house, Nickel had pretty much decided to walk to school. Riding his bike would just be asking for trouble, and he was getting enough of that without asking. He wondered if the guys would follow him home today, what he would do if they did. Wondered if Pop would wait and watch again. He couldn't keep doing that for the whole school year.

Then Nickel saw the bike and forgot everything else. The rusty, dented bicycle he had been working on yesterday stood sleek, black, shining in the sunlight so that it almost hurt to look at it. He approached, touched the gleaming metal, felt the warmth of it under his hand.

The bike seemed larger, it looked powerful, and Nickel thought of his struggle with it last night, in the rain and darkness. It had seemed different then, it looked different now, beyond what rust remover and polish could do. But right now Nickel didn't care about that. All he wanted to do was ride the bike, see how it handled, what it could do. It looked like it could do anything.

They headed down the lane, smooth and quiet, no rattles or bumps. But it wasn't an easy ride. The bike moved fast, much quicker than Nickel was comfortable with, and he seemed to brake more than he pedaled. Nickel found himself fighting, and the bike seemed to be fighting back. He felt disappointed. The ride that should be so much fun wasn't, and it was his fault. The bike was too much for him, he couldn't handle it. He was afraid of it. As they rode down the old road and into the development, the bike seemed to slow down, to lose its energy, almost as if it felt disappointment, too.

Nickel had been looking forward to riding up to the school like a king, showing off, enjoying the sight of the kids' jaws dropping when they saw his bike. But not now. He saw kids staring, but he couldn't take any pleasure in it, just left the bike in the parking lot and walked away feeling guilty, feeling like he'd let somebody down.

Several kids asked him about the bike, where he'd gotten it, and when he said it wasn't a new one, they wanted to know what he'd done to it. "Just cleaned it up," was all he could tell them. It wasn't the whole story, but he didn't know what the whole story was. He felt sort of down, the day seemed to drag.

Logan and Tyler had heard about Nickel trying to run Robbo down in the parking lot, just laughed when he told them the bike did it. He had to laugh, too, thinking about Robbo on the ground with that incredulous look on his face, and then they *really* thought he had done it on purpose; he couldn't change their minds. He knew he'd never be able to change Robbo's mind, either, and he began to feel a little apprehensive. He'd been so excited about the bike this morning that nothing else had seemed to matter much, but now he began to think about what revenge plans Robbo might be hatching.

The other boys were thinking about it, too. Tyler said, "Aren't you afraid Robbo will get somebody to take your bike, like he did your other one?"

"It's locked up," Nickel said. "I didn't do that before."

"That's no guarantee," Logan said. "He's probably got a locksmith working on it right now."

"Yeah, or a safecracker," Tyler said.

"Yeah, or an explosives expert," Logan said.

"Right," Nickel said. "He's going to blow up the whole parking lot just to get my bike."

"You know Robbo," Logan said.

"Yeah," Nickel said. "I wish I didn't."

Nickel left school, saw his bike was okay, then wondered why they were all so worried about it. It was the bike *rider* Robbo had it in for.

They moved in on him as he unlocked the bike. At the same time, Nickel felt a prickly sensation in his hands. He looked at his palms curiously, but there was nothing to see. Then he realized that the feeling was coming through the bike. A series of little electric shocks was surging out of the handlebars, running up his arms. He'd felt something like it before, but not this strong.

He didn't fight it when Justin and Dodger grabbed his arms, when Robbo snatched the bike away. Some of the other kids saw what was going on. One or two even looked as if they might come over and help Nickel, but he wasn't looking for help. He was watching Robbo, wondering if he could sense the life in the bike, if he could sense the danger. Nickel's palms still felt the warmth, his fingers tingled.

If Robbo noticed anything, it didn't show. He walked the bike a short distance away, turned to face Nickel and smiled. "Let's see how *you* like getting run down." He put one foot on the pedal, threw his other leg over the bike. Justin and Dodger held on to Nickel, ready to run out of the way at the last minute. But there was nothing to run from. The bike didn't move, not the expected way. Instead it went flat on its side, taking Robbo with it. He got up quickly, looked around viciously to see if anyone was laughing, tried again to get going, fell again. Nickel watched in fascination.

Everybody in the parking lot was watching. Robbo made another attempt, failed again, and Nickel thought he knew how he was feeling. He couldn't give up. The whole school would be laughing at him if he didn't ride that bike. He had to keep trying. But he couldn't stay on. The bike wouldn't let him.

Justin and Dodger let go of Nickel, walked away as if they were embarrassed to be a part of what was happening to Robbo, or scared.

Finally Robbo did it, managed to get the bike moving while he perched on the seat looking desperate and determined. He got his balance, steered in a big circle to get up speed, and then headed directly toward Nickel. Some of the kids yelled at Nickel to run, but he didn't need to run. Nickel knew Robbo well enough to be afraid of him, to know that he was a dangerous enemy. But Robbo was riding Nickel's bike, and Nickel knew he didn't have to be afraid of the bike.

There was time for a few seconds of doubt, though, as Robbo rode faster, got closer—and then suddenly Robbo was in the air, legs kicking, hands grabbing at space, and then on the ground, landing with a thud at Nickel's feet.

Nickel knew better than to hang around. He jumped over Robbo, grabbed the bike before it fell, and took off.

The trouble was, the bike didn't seem to want to go.

It made quick spurts ahead, then sudden slowdowns, and Nickel wondered if it would send him flying the way it did Robbo. The bike didn't scare him the way it had this morning. This ride was more like a battle of wills, and Nickel was determined to win. He was in a sweat when he got home, tired, excited, blisters on his hands from squeezing the handlebars. He barreled up the lane, skidded in a big circle before he came to a stop.

Pop was working on the tractor, but he put down his wrench, came over to Nickel. Looked at the bike, sort of whistled under his breath. "What have you got there?"

Nickel looked at it, too, couldn't quite say what he was thinking, finally just said, "I don't know."

When Joe got home and saw the bike, his eyes bugged out. "Where'd you get the paint?"

Nickel said what he'd been saying all day. "I just cleaned it up."

"You did more than that." Joe rubbed his hand over the fenders, the frame. "It doesn't seem like the same bike."

Pop put an arm around Nickel's shoulders, nodded toward the bike. "Looks good, don't it?"

"The kid is some bike cleaner," Joe said. "How's it ride since we fixed it up?"

No use telling him. No way to describe the ride. No way to describe the feeling. Nickel said, "It's not like any other bike."

"Let me give it a try." Before Nickel could say anything, Joe was on the bike. But not going anywhere. He tried to push off, but the pedals didn't move. He stood with one foot on the ground while he kicked at the pedal with his other foot. "What's going on?" he said.

Nickel felt a little nervous. He was thinking of Robbo's ride, or his attempt, hoping the bike wouldn't pull anything like that with Joe.

"I think it needs a little more work before you ride it," he told Joe, but Joe said, "You rode it, didn't you?"

"Well, it's more used to me." Nickel explained.

Joe hopped along on one foot, pushed a pedal with the other, but no luck. "It's a bike," he said. "It doesn't care who rides it." But the pedal refused to turn.

"Seems like this one cares," Pop said.

Joe gave up, let the bike drop. "I don't have time to fool with this now." He headed for the house.

Nickel picked up the bike, wheeled it over to the back steps, ran his hands along the handlebars. He looked over at Pop. Their glances held for a second before they went into the house.

Joe and Starla had news. They broke it at the dinner table. Joe had a job offer back where they lived before. They were leaving.

The news hit Nickel hard. He didn't say a word, just sat there stiff as a stick, listening to their excited talk. Mom looked interested, asked questions, didn't seem to care that he was going away. Pop didn't say anything. Nothing. They were just going to let him go.

A band seemed to wrap around Nickel's throat, squeeze tighter and tighter until suddenly the word he had to say broke through, and he stood up, ignored the glass he knocked over, choked, "No!"

"Look what you did," Starla said, trying to stop the milk from running onto the floor.

Mom got up, grabbed a towel to sop up the mess. "Sit down, Nickel, what's the matter with you? Don't you want to see Josiah and Starla get ahead?"

Nickel sat down. "I'm not going," he said.

"Of course you're not," Mom said. Rinsed the towel. Spread it on the dish drainer. Sat down at the table and looked around. "He's not," she said.

Nickel heard Pop take a deep breath. So he'd been worried, too.

Starla said, "No, he's our responsibility," and Joe said, "We didn't bring him here to dump him on you."

Mom said, "He's staying."

Then Joe said, "What does Pop say?"

Pop took his time answering, finally said, "With him here I can put in another couple acres of corn."

Nickel grinned. "Three against two," he said.

Starla looked at Joe, said, "It's nice here, a nice place to grow up." Joe said, "If you like living where nothing ever happens." Nickel relaxed. It was settled.

Nickel and Pop spent the evening talking about the new barn, what could be used, what had to be rebuilt. Nickel had a lot of ideas, most of them not much good because he didn't know enough about the farm business yet, but sometimes he got an approving look from Pop for something he said. That felt good. Joe was disgusted, or pretended to be, told Starla he never would have brought the kid here if he'd known he'd turn into a farmer.

Nickel was in bed, but not ready to sleep. He wanted to think about how different everything was now that he knew he was going to stay here with the Clendaniels. This was his own bed now, his own room. The house was his house, the farm was his farm, Mom and Pop were his family. He fought sleep, felt himself drifting off anyway. In a half dream he saw Cougar, the way he had come from nowhere, running by the car that first night. Like he'd been waiting. Not for Joe, though. For Nickel. He woke up with a little jump, knowing Cougar had been in his mind, not sure what were thoughts and what was dream.

He got out of bed, went to the window, looked out hopefully. It was just last night that he had seen

Cougar out there in the rainy darkness, and for the space of a heartbeat, Nickel almost thought he was standing there again. But it wasn't a horse waiting for him by the barn. It was the bike.

Chapter 15

Nickel left the house the next morning and jumped on the bicycle feeling ready for anything. The bike seemed ready for anything, too. Maybe a little too ready. It aimed straight for the fence, gathering speed as if it would jump right over it. Nickel held tight, forced the handlebars to turn, kept the wheels going down the lane. Once they got out on the road he made himself relax, trust the bike instead of fighting it, stop trying to slow it down. And that made all the difference. In contrast to the jerky, shaky ride he'd had yesterday, this one was smooth as silk. It was only when the bike showed signs of heading off the road that things got a little rough, but Nickel was beginning to understand the bike, to learn how to get what he wanted from it. He felt in control now, and yesterday's disappointing ride was history. He rode into the parking lot knowing that Robbo would be after him today, maybe during school, maybe after, but he didn't feel scared anymore. If trouble came, he had a family to back him up. And he had his bike.

* * *

Robbo, Justin, and Dodger rode slowly into the parking lot, side by side. They all had pretty fancy bikes, at least until you saw them next to Nickel's. No bike could look good next to Nickel's. They must have been watching for him, planned their entrance to start him worrying. They came up to him like outlaws riding into town in an old cowboy movie, rode around him in a tight circle, giving him tough movie-outlaw looks. It was sort of impressive. Then it got silly. Robbo gave Nickel an extra-tough look and said, "Later, chump," before he rode away, so of course Justin and Dodger had to do the same thing. They meant to be scary, but they were just funny, and instead of worrying about later, Nickel couldn't wait to describe the scene to Logan and Tyler. He knew that all day they would answer everything with, "Later, chump."

In case Nickel hadn't gotten the point in the parking lot, Robbo got close to him in gym, started to say something. Nickel had already told Tyler about this morning, and right now he regretted it. Robbo was mad enough. He didn't need to be any madder. But Tyler was behind him, jumping up and down like a gorilla and mouthing the words, "Later, chump." Nickel didn't want to watch, didn't want to laugh, but he did both. Robbo swung around to see what was going on and, that quick, Tyler stopped being a gorilla, just stood there with a goofy smile on his face.

Robbo glared at Nickel, looked undecided, finally snorted and walked away.

"Why do you do things like that?" Nickel asked. "He was so mad I could hear the circuits in his brain shorting out."

"Look who's talking," Tyler said. "The kid who rammed Robbo with his bike one day and knocked him off it the next."

"It wasn't like that," Nickel protested. "I never look for trouble, you know that. I'm not as crazy as you are."

"I like to think of it as being brave," Tyler said. "Of course, knowing I'll be safe on the bus after school doesn't hurt."

"Well, everything that happened to Robbo was an accident," Nickel said, and Tyler said, "Right, Nick. I'd like to hear you explaining it all to Robbo."

In the cafeteria Logan said, "Maybe you shouldn't go home alone today. Maybe you should call somebody to come and get you."

Nickel considered, said, "He could just be trying to scare me."

"He's already jumped you once," Logan said.

"And Robbo doesn't say 'Later, chump' for nothing," Tyler said.

He and Logan laughed, but they were serious, too, and Nickel felt their worry starting to rub off on him. It looked like Robbo really was going to come after him. Not alone, of course; he never did anything alone. This morning it hadn't seemed to matter. Nickel had felt like he could handle anything. He had the world's most outstanding bike. And he had a family to look out for him. But his family wasn't here. Robbo was.

So they made plans. When the bell rang, Nickel would beat it out of there, and Logan and Tyler would do something to slow Robbo down, give Nickel a head start, even if it was only a few seconds. "We'll create a diversion," Logan said. They all liked the phrase. It sounded important, like they really had a plan.

Every time they looked over at Robbo, he seemed to be looking Nickel's way. Or else deep in talk with Dodger and Justin.

"What could they be talking about?" Nickel said. "How much planning does it take to beat somebody to a pulp?"

"They're probably arguing over who gets which part," Logan said.

"Wait, I'll read their lips," Tyler said. "Yeah, Robbo just said, 'I'll flatten his head,' and Justin said, 'I'll rip off his arms,' and now Dodger's saying—"

"Shut up, Tyler," Logan said. "You can't read lips."

"He's probably right, though," Nickel said. "I bet that's exactly what they're saying."

"Don't worry, Nick," Logan said. "They don't know about our diversion."

"That's right," Tyler said. "We're going to create a diversion like they've never seen. The diversion of the year. The diversion of the century."

Nickel and Logan looked at him. "Tyler," Nickel said, "are you sure you know what a diversion is?"

By the end of the day Nickel was tense, scared, watching the clock, and ready to run. His calm mood of the morning was gone. He didn't want to get beaten up. He didn't want the trouble that would come from it.

At the first chirp of the bell, Nickel made a dash for the door and kept going. He could hear scuffling behind him, pictured Tyler and Logan blocking the doorway, getting in everyone's way, creating their diversion. He ran outside, messed up the lock combination, had to do it again, and by then kids were streaming out the door. He jumped on the bike, started out of the parking lot, looked over his shoulder to see Robbo and the others running for their bikes.

Robbo, Justin, and Dodger fell in behind him, and Nickel saw that they were going to follow him, probably down to the old road where they could take him apart away from the eyes of teachers or anybody else who might interfere. But Tyler and Logan's diversion had given him an edge. Nickel had a good chance of getting home ahead of them. They wouldn't follow him up the farm lane, wouldn't jump him in his own yard, not in broad daylight.

Something was wrong, though. He knew his bike was faster than any of those following him. But they were gaining. He stood up, brought all his weight down on the pedals, but the gap between him and the others lessened. Then he felt the bike turning, as if it didn't want to run away, as if it wanted to face what was coming after them. But Nickel didn't want to face them. There were too many.

"No!" He pulled with all his strength on the handlebars, swinging them to the front again. "Go, Cougar!" he yelled.

The bike shuddered beneath him—he felt it under his hands, up his arms, through his legs—and then it leaped forward, jerking Nickel's head back, almost throwing him from his seat. His feet found the pedals again, he clutched the handlebars, leaned low. The road came toward him so fast it made him dizzy. On either side the leaves were an orange blur. He risked a look behind him, saw that he had left the others in his dust, not just Robbo and his boys, but other kids, too. There were at least ten bikes following him. Nosy kids. By now the whole school knew what was going on.

Well, they were going to be disappointed. He had reached the farm lane, way ahead of the pack. He was safe, for today anyway. He braked, turned the wheel, expecting to enter the lane. The tire slid sideways, scraped along the road, raised dust, leaves, gravel. But the bike didn't turn, and in an instant it was too late. Nickel straightened the handlebars, pointed the wheel forward again before the bike could overturn. He didn't understand what had just happened, but there was nothing else to do but hang on.

He looked back again to see how much of a lead he had, but they had rounded a bend in the road, there was nothing to see. Up ahead, the ground on the right sloped upward and a washed-out driveway led to a weather-beaten old barn. Nickel hadn't planned it, but the bike turned sharply, flew up the drive and through the big door that hung open on broken hinges. It slid across old hay and corncobs to the far end of the barn, skidded around to face the door, and stopped. Nickel put one foot on the floor for balance and waited.

It was dark in the barn, except where sunlight shot through a dusty window, through pinholes in the roof. It was silent, except for the fluttering and cooing of pigeons in the rafters. Then there were sounds from outside, distant at first and then louder, bike tires on leaves and gravel, kids' voices, and Nickel felt the tremors again. From pedals to seat to handlebars, they flashed through the bike, through Nickel. This time he was ready, and when the bike took off, he was a part of it. They roared across the dark barn and rocketed out the door into the sunshine, into the midst of the kids, Nickel yelling, laughing with excitement.

The kids scattered in all directions, but it was the

leaders that the bike headed for. Justin tried to turn back, lost control, went spinning one way, his bike another. Dodger, his eyes on Nickel instead of the road, hit a rock, pitched over his handlebars and crashed to the ground.

Robbo threw his bike aside, made a run for it, tried to get off the road, into the rough field where a bike couldn't go. But the bike caught up with him at the ditch along the road, and Robbo shouted and threw himself facedown, protecting his head with his arms. Nickel saw him cowering below them as the bike jumped the ditch and then took the fence, just sailed right over it, and raced across the field. There was another fence, another field, and by now Nickel wasn't thinking of anything, not of the bad old days, not of the trouble with Robbo. There was only sun and space and speed. He had outrun the world. And then there was another fence, and the lane, and home, and Pop waiting for them by the barn.

At school the story went around that, when the bike came out of the barn, smoke and flames were shooting out of it. Nickel always laughed when anybody said that, but he didn't deny it. Just because he hadn't seen it didn't mean it hadn't happened.

Now all the schoolkids wanted to know him, everybody wanted to be able to say he was a friend. Even Dodger and Justin acted important, bragged about being knocked down by the wild bike. Robbo didn't brag, though. He knew that his days of being in charge were over. He had to get used to being an ordinary kid like everybody else, athletic but not the best, tough but not the toughest.

The kids at school couldn't leave the bike alone. Somebody was always examining it, asking questions about it. They all wanted to know how it could do the things it did. They all wanted one just like it. Nickel never talked about it, never tried to explain. He couldn't. He didn't understand it himself, and if Pop had any ideas, he wasn't talking.

Nickel thought that sometime he'd like to tell somebody what he knew, what he thought. Maybe Lisa. She'd listen, take it seriously, have ideas about it. But for now, it was enough for Nickel to be free to play sports, to joke around, to go where he wanted without worrying about who was waiting for him. And to know that at home there was someone looking out for him. That was all he'd ever wanted anyway. But being a school hero, having a bike that was a school legend—well, that just made it all that much better.